Edwin Speaks Up

WRITTEN BY April Stevens ILLUSTRATED BY Sophie Blackall

schwartz & wade books • new york

Gloo poop SHOE noogie froo KEY

To my mom—A.S.

For Ann, Flavio, Lucia and Emilio—S.B.

 Published in the United States by Schwartz & Wade Books,
an imprint of Random House Children's Books, a division of Random House, Inc., New York.
Schwartz & Wade Books and the colophon are trademarks of Random House, Inc.

Visit us on the Web! www.randomhouse.com/kids
Educators and librarians, for a variety of teaching tools,
visit us at www.randomhouse.com/teachers

Library of Congress Cataloging-in-Publication Data
Stevens, April. Edwin speaks up / April Stevens; illustrated by Sophie Blackall.—1st ed. p. cm.
Summary: Before his family leaves the grocery store, Baby Edwin makes sure their grocery cart contains the last ingredient needed to make his birthday celebration complete.
ISBN 978-0-375-85337-1 (trade) — ISBN 978-0-375-95633-1 (Gibraltar lib. bdg.) [1. Babies—Fiction. 2. Birthdays—Fiction. 3. Grocery shopping—Fiction.
4. Family life—Fiction. 5. Humorous stories.] I. Title. PZ7.S84315Bb 2010 [E]—dc22 2009028009

The text of this book is set in Berling. The illustrations were made using Chinese ink, watercolor, and gouache on Arches hot press paper.
Book design by Rachael Cole

MANUFACTURED IN MALAYSIA • 10 9 8 7 6 5 4 3 2 1 • First Edition

SUGAR
SUGAR
SUGAR
SUGAR

Mrs. Finnemore was racing around the house.

"Gloo poop SHOE noogie froo KEY," Baby Edwin was babbling. He was all dressed and ready to go to the supermarket.

"Mommmmmy," Finney whined. "Can't we just *go*?"

Suddenly Mrs. Finnemore stopped short.

"Oh, for Pete's sake, there they are!" she said, and she reached into Fergus's shoe on the hall table and pulled out her car keys.

It was a fine day as Mrs. Finnemore and her five children trooped down the front steps and out to their old car.

"I call the front seat!" Fergus hollered.

"But Mommmmy," Franny complained, "Fergus *always* gets the front seat."

"Fergus," Mrs. Finnemore said, putting her hand on her hip. "You'll sit in the back today."

She plopped Edwin into his car seat.

Then she started up the engine and backed down the driveway.

"Figbutton noo noo POCKY BOOKY froppin ROOF," Edwin babbled.

"Now, children, we absolutely mustn't forget the sugar for Edwin's birthday cake tomorrow," Mrs. Finnemore said, and turned out onto Horatio Avenue.

"I'm hot! Franny, open your window," Finney shouted.

"Mom, tell Franny to close her window. My hair's blowing," Fergus hollered.

HORATIO AVE

Once they'd parked at Fineson's Fine Grocery, Mrs. Finnemore looked around the car. "Oh dear, I forgot my pocketbook," she said.

All the Finnemore children groaned.

"Frigle dee ROOFY plowck." Edwin kicked his little feet.

Frigle dee RoOFY plowck

Just then Mr. Caruso, who'd been loading his groceries nearby, tapped on Mrs. Finnemore's window. "Pardon me," he said, and pointed. "Perhaps you should check your roof."

Mrs. Finnemore looked up. "Well, what do you know!" She laughed and marched into Fineson's Fine Grocery.

FINESONS'
FINESONS'
FINE GROCER

Mrs. Finnemore had her keys, her pocketbook, her list and her children. She plunked Baby Edwin into the shopping cart and started off up aisle number one.

"Children," she announced. "Remember, your job is to not forget the sugar for Edwin's birthday cake."

"Clob foo poop SWEETY," Edwin babbled.

1
Clob foo poop
SWEETY

Mrs. Finnemore began throwing apples, pears, grapes and bananas into the cart.

Fiona climbed on the back.

"It's MY turn!" Franny screeched, and yanked Fiona off.

"But I just got on! MOMMMMMY, make her stop," Fiona howled.

Mrs. Finnemore was bagging string beans, grabbing broccoli and clutching cucumbers.

FRESH
Gloody pooper do no LEAVEY

“Let’s see, what’s next on my list?” she murmured.

“Gloody pooper do no LEAVEY.” Edwin kicked his little feet as Mrs. Finnemore rounded aisle number two, heading for the cracker section.

"Did someone take my cart?" Mrs. Finnemore could hear Mrs. Lutzheimer call from aisle number one.

"However could someone lose their cart?" Mrs. Finnemore clucked and shook her head as she turned into aisle three. "Now, children, make sure to get that sugar."

SUGAR
SUGAR
SUGAR
SUGAR
SUGAR
3
15¢

"Doon weewee fleetum FASTY!" Mrs. Finnemore heard Edwin giggle in the next aisle.

"Oh my, where has Baby Edwin got to?" she said.

Suddenly Mrs. Lutzheimer rounded the corner.

"Excuse me, but I believe you have my cart," she said.

"Oh, and I believe you have my Edwin!" Mrs. Finnemore laughed, shook her head and gave Baby Edwin a little kiss.

Mrs. Lutzheimer took her cart and waved goodbye to Edwin.

SUGAR

ICE CREAM

"Rootin popel CART no no SWEETY," Edwin said as all the Finnemores rolled toward the ice cream section.

"I want chocolate," Fergus announced.

"Mommmmy," Fiona moaned. "I don't like chocolate!"

"Edwin, darling, what flavor ice cream would you like with your cake?" asked Mrs. Finnemore.

All four Finnemore children turned and looked at their little brother.

"Gimpin chalk lil wizz um SWEETIN' do a bye bye."
Edwin pointed across the store.

"I think he said chocolate," Fergus said.

"He said vanilla," Fiona insisted.

Mrs. Finnemore gave a little shrug and threw a pint of each into the cart. Then off they all rolled to the checkout.

77
00000
SWEETUM No No!

"Plopin grouff shooop CAKE sweet NO NO," Edwin said.

Franny took the ice cream out of the cart and put it on the checkout belt.

"SWEETUM NO NO!" he said a little louder.

"Oh, Edwin honey, is your diaper wet?" Mrs. Finnemore sighed.

Fergus leaned in for the macaroni.

"Now, isn't it a perfect day?" Mrs. Finnemore chatted with the cashier as she began ringing up her groceries.

Fiona grabbed the broccoli.

Finney begged Mrs. Finnemore for gum.

But Baby Edwin was quiet.

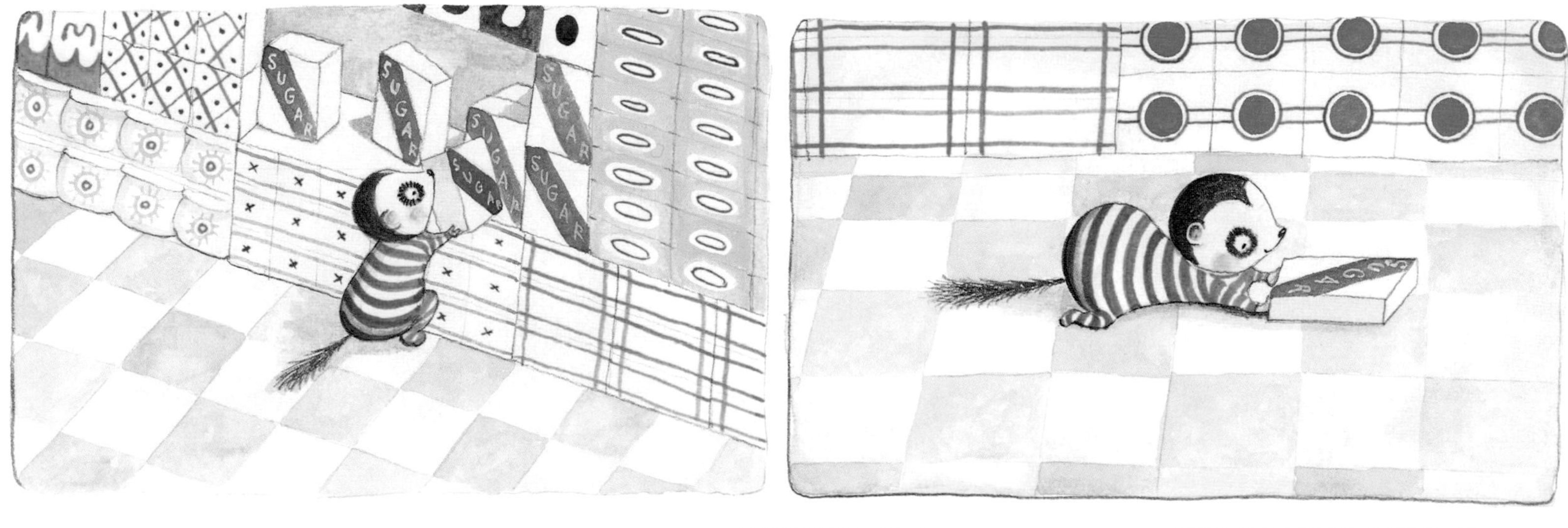

And just as Mrs. Finnemore reached for her pocketbook to pay, Baby Edwin dropped one large box of sugar onto the belt.

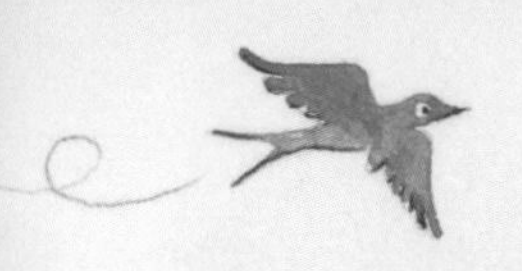

It was still a fine day as the Finnemores came out of Fineson's Fine Grocery. Edwin looked up into the sky. "Pople goo goo BIRD dooola looopy," he said.

pople goo goo
BIRD dooola
looopy

The family piled into their old blue car and Mrs. Finnemore started the engine.

"Roofum sweet," Baby Edwin babbled.

Mrs. Finnemore looked at her youngest and shook her head. "Tomorrow is Baby Edwin's birthday—he's growing up so fast. Soon he'll be talking. Can you *even* imagine that?"

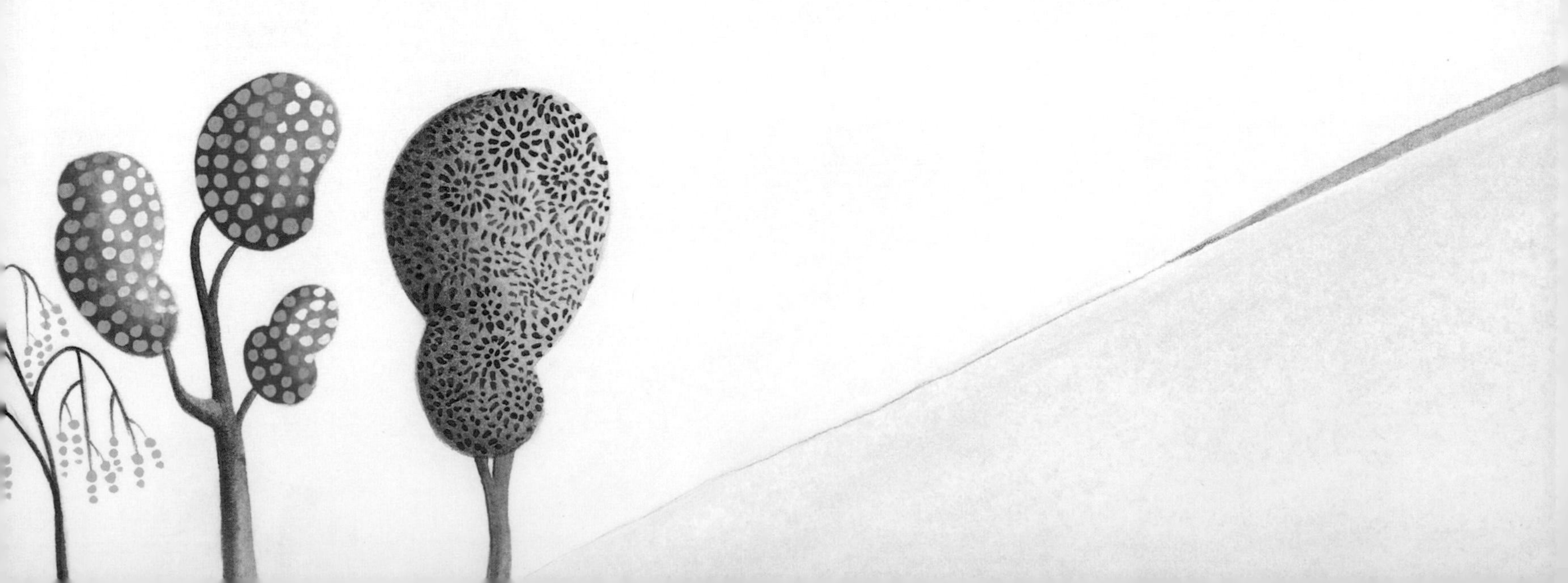

Roofum sweet

SUGAR
SUGAR
SUGAR
SUGAR